Little Red Hen Gets Help

Little Red Hen
Gets Help

Kenneth Spengler

Illustrated by
Margaret Spengler

Green Light Readers
Harcourt, Inc.
Orlando   Austin   New York
San Diego   Toronto   London

One day, Little Red Hen got up.
She was hungry.

"Who wants to eat this?" she asked.

"Not I," said Cat.
"I can't," said Fox.
"Oh, no," said Pig.

"Who wants some tacos?"
asked Little Red Hen.

"I do!" they all yelled.

"Will you help make tacos?"

"Yes!" said Cat.
"I will!" said Fox.
"Let me, too!" said Pig.

Little Red Hen fed Cat, Fox, and Pig.

"What a mess! Who will pick up?"

"Not I," said Cat.
"I can't," said Fox.
"Oh, no," said Pig.

"We will help!" called the ants.

"Thank you, ants," said Little Red Hen.
"Next time, I will ask you first!"

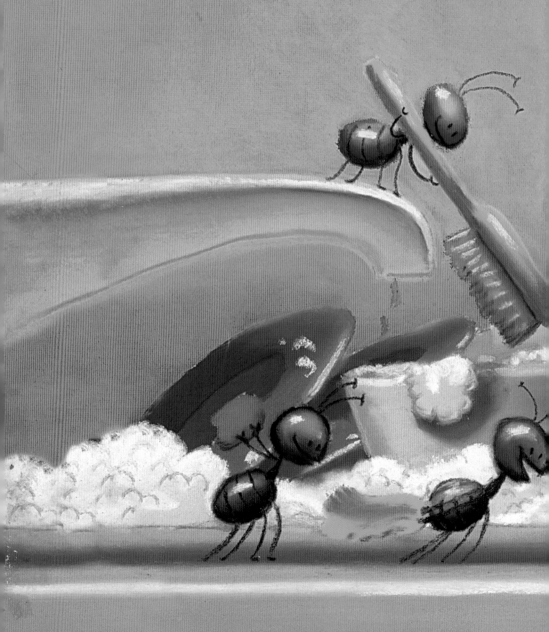

Collage Animals

Make collage animals and tell a story about them.

You will need:

ribbons

cloth scraps

construction paper

glue

buttons

glitter

feathers

scissors

markers

crayons

- Choose an animal that you like.

- Use different materials to make that animal.

- Try a few different things before you glue the materials.

- When you finish your animal collage, write a story about your animal.

- Then share your story with a group.

Meet the Author
Kenneth Spengler

Kenneth Spengler likes to write funny stories.
He worked with his wife, Margaret, on this one.

"I enjoyed writing this story because I love food,
especially tacos! Just like Little Red Hen, I like
to have help when I make a meal. Sometimes we
spill food on the floor. Our dog, Jackie, helps
clean it up, though, not ants!"

Meet the Illustrator
Margaret Spengler

Margaret Spengler is the artist who made
the pictures for this story. She painted them
on sandpaper with pastel chalk and water.
The thing she likes best about being an artist
is the creativity.

"I like Little Red Hen because she is smart
and caring. I also like the way she shares with
her friends."

Requests for permission to make copies of any part of the work should be submitted online
at www.harcourt.com/contact or mailed to the following address: Permissions Department,
Harcourt, Inc., 6277 Sea Harbor Drive, Orlando, Florida 32887-6777.

www.HarcourtBooks.com

First Green Light Readers edition 2007

Green Light Readers is a trademark of Harcourt, Inc., registered in the
United States of America and/or other jurisdictions.

Library of Congress Cataloging-in-Publication Data
Spengler, Kenneth.
Little Red Hen gets help/Kenneth Spengler; illustrated by Margaret Spengler.
p. cm.
"Green Light Readers."
Summary: When Little Red Hen makes tacos, cat, Fox, and
Pig want to eat, but they do not want to help clean up.
[1. Folklore.] I. Spengler, Margaret, ill. II. Little red hen. English. III. Title.
PZ8.1.S743Lit 2007
398.2—dc22
[E]   2006038684
ISBN 978-0-15-206195-1
ISBN 978-0-15-206189-0 (pb)

A C E G H F D B
A C E G H F D B (pb)

Ages 5–7
Grade: 1
Guided Reading Level: D
Reading Recovery Level: 5

Green Light Readers
For the reader who's ready to GO!

"A must-have for any family with a beginning reader."—*Boston Sunday Herald*

"You can't go wrong with adding several copies of these terrific books to your beginning-to-read collection."—*School Library Journal*

"A winner for the beginner."—*Booklist*

Five Tips to Help Your Child Become a Great Reader

1. Get involved. Reading aloud to and with your child is just as important as encouraging your child to read independently.

2. Be curious. Ask questions about what your child is reading.

3. Make reading fun. Allow your child to pick books on subjects that interest her or him.

4. Words are everywhere—not just in books. Practice reading signs, packages, and cereal boxes with your child.

5. Set a good example. Make sure your child sees YOU reading.

Why Green Light Readers Is the Best Series for Your New Reader

● Created exclusively for beginning readers by some of the biggest and brightest names in children's books

● Reinforces the reading skills your child is learning in school

● Encourages children to read—and finish—books by themselves

● Offers extra enrichment through fun, age-appropriate activities unique to each story

● Incorporates characteristics of the Reading Recovery program used by educators

● Developed with Harcourt School Publishers and credentialed educational consultants

Look for more Green Light Readers wherever books are sold!